Miss Dooley

Bubbles can take
us anywhere —
what fun adventures
await us.

Have fun reading!

Diane Terry

May
2011

Published by Oren Village, LLC, Battle Creek, Michigan.
For information or permission to reproduce, please contact
Diane Terry @ dianeterryauthor.com.
Text set in Baskerville. Cover design by Libby Carruth Krock.
Illustrations rendered in pencil, acrylic paint and pastel.

PUBLISHER'S CATALOGING-IN-PUBLICATION DATA

Terry, Diane.

The bubble gum fairy / written by Diane Terry & Kalee Bartko ;
illustrated by Rachel K. Ackerman. -- Battle Creek, MI : Oren Village,
c2009.

p. ; cm.
ISBN: 978-0-9777272-4-7
Audience: Grades K-5.
Summary: Moving to a new town without any friends has Kalee
feeling blue. But that's all about to change thanks to a tiny fairy and
a very special gum ball. Maybe Bloomingdale isn't so bad after all.

1. Moving, Household--Juvenile fiction. 2. Friendship--Juvenile
fiction. 3. Fairies--Juvenile fiction. 4. Bubble gum--Juvenile fiction.
5. [Moving, Household--Fiction. 6. Friendship--Fiction. 7. Fairies--
Fiction. 8. Bubble gum--Fiction.] I. Bartko, Kalee. II. Ackerman,
Rachel K. III. Title.

Printed in Korea

PZ7.T279 B83 2009
[Fic]--dc22   0905

THE BUBBLE GUM Fairy

By Diane Terry & Kalee Bartko   Illustrations By Rachel K. Ackerman

To all dreamers
who dare to make their dreams come true!

Special Thanks To:

Alan St. Jean for all his help!
-D. Terry

My family and Dr. Dominic Catalano for seeing my potential!
-R. Ackerman

Kalee had lived in Bloomingdale for a month already, yet she had not made a friend.

Today, as she walked by the park on her way to the candy store, she saw kids playing soccer. "I wish I could play too!" she said to herself.

Crack! Boom!

Her thoughts were interrupted by a clap of thunder, so she ran the rest of the way to the candy store. Reaching into her pocket, Kalee found two quarters and a dime! One thought was on her mind…bubble gum! She raced to the machine, put in a quarter, turned the handle, and hoped for a blue one!

Meanwhile in Fairytown, the pixies were mixing the kettles of blue bubble gum. The Bubble Gum Fairy went to the magic mirror and spoke.

"Chew, chew, blow a bubble,
Soon she will be out of trouble,
Crack! Snap! I have begun
To change a life with bubble gum!"

Pop!

Click! Rrrr! Kalee heard her gumball rolling down the chute. She lifted the red door and peeked inside. There, dusting herself off was a little fairy.

"Aaachoo!" The fairy sneezed from all the bubble gum dust!

"But…how?" murmured Kalee.

"Hello, my dear, how do you do?
May I introduce myself to you?
I'm jolly, fun, and oh so merry,
I'm known as the Bubble Gum Fairy."

Kalee stood there stunned! The fairy continued.

"I have planned an exciting day
Step right up, come this way!
Blowing bubbles is such fun,
Let me show you how it's done!"

The Bubble Gum Fairy tapped her wings and a blue gumball appeared.

"The flavor's great, the gum is too.
Now listen, here is what you do.
Chew your gum to twice its size,
It might take a couple tries."

Kalee blew a bubble and it popped all over her face! The Bubble Gum Fairy giggled,

"Not bad, my dear, not bad at all
Chew one more for a bigger ball.
Shape the bubble with your hand,
Blow it slowly, make it grand!"

Kalee put another piece of gum in her mouth. Her next bubble was gigantic!
"I didn't know there were tricks to blowing good bubbles!" Kalee said excitedly.

"You're blowing bubbles awfully well,
Now it's time to cast my spell.
Carriage bubble, twist and twirl
I summon for this little girl!"

Kalee practiced taking several deep breaths and then she blew with all her might. The next bubble was enormous! The Bubble Gum Fairy took the bubble from Kalee's mouth and set it on the ground.

"Well done, I'm proud of you!
Now bubble double again times two
Tap! Tap! Grow bubble grow!
Kalee's got somewhere to go!"

Shaking her head in disbelief, Kalee walked toward the magnificent bubble. The Bubble Gum Fairy smiled,

"Now it's time to take your ride
Won't you please step inside?
Blowing bubbles sure is fun
But wait until you ride in one!"

"I'd love to," said Kalee, "I just wish I had some friends to go with me."

"I understand, I do indeed
A friend or two is what you need.
To the soccer field we go,
There you'll find some friends to know."

The Bubble Gum Fairy tapped her wings and the two were soon magically floating in the bubble.

The rain had stopped and ribbons of rainbow color crossed the sky as the bubble landed at the soccer field.

The Bubble Gum Fairy stepped out and announced:

"We're going on a magic ride,
Who would like to step inside?
Enter through the light blue door
You'll be changed forever more."

Only two children, a boy and a girl, heard the strange invitation.

"Where did that huge bubble come from?" gasped the girl.
"Who cares?" the boy shouted, "Let's go!"
Kalee welcomed them into the bubble. It quickly lifted into the air.
"I've never been this high! Look how small everything is! This is awesome!" giggled the little girl. "By the way, I'm Jessica. This is my brother Joshua."
"I'm Kalee. Glad to meet you."
"Where are we going?" asked Joshua.
"I wish we could ride over the rainbow!" exclaimed Kalee.

A gust of wind blew their bubble through several droplets of rain and as the sun's rays glistened, a rainbow appeared! Each of the colored stripes had such a wonderful scent!

The Bubble Gum Fairy turned proudly towards the children.

"My pixies gather from this bow,
Special flavors that you know.
Orange, lemon, lime, and cherry,
Banana, grape, and blue raspberry.

They pour the flavors, oh so sweet,
Into kettles and stir the treat.
The magic taste is so delicious,
Those who chew it get their wishes."

"I wish we could spend an entire day here!" yelled Jessica.
"Me, too!" shouted Joshua.
Tap! Tap! The magic door opened. Out they ran!

Then with a nod from the Bubble Gum Fairy, Kalee and her friends knew it was time to go. They ran swiftly back into the bubble, lifted off, and drifted amidst the clouds. Suddenly the bubble wall began to collapse.

"Help!" cried Jessica, "The bubble is caving in! What should we do?"

The Bubble Gum Fairy spoke calmly,

"The heat of the sun is melting the wall
But do not worry! You will not fall.
We'll land in just a minute or two,
Relax. I will take care of you."

Tap, tap went her wings.

The odd shaped bubble drifted quickly to the ground and popped! Joshua, Jessica, and Kalee found themselves standing by the candy store.

"Kalee, that was fantastic! What a day this has been!" said Joshua. "Would you like to come to the soccer field and play?"

A smile crossed Kalee's face.

"Oh, and I'm having a birthday party on Friday at six," said Jessica. "Please come!"

"I'd love to!" said Kalee.

Kalee turned around to thank the Bubble Gum Fairy for the best day of her life, but she was nowhere to be found.

Back in Fairytown, standing in front of the mirror at the bubble gum factory, the Bubble Gum Fairy watched Kalee walk back to the soccer field with her new friends. She smiled and said,

"Blow a bubble big and blue,
Step inside, see dreams come true.
Today Kalee found some friends,
That is how our story ends."

Then the Bubble Gum Fairy took off her wings, put up her feet, and ate some chocolate.